SOME GREYS

Nothing's Ever Black & White

Isiah J. Pringle

TO THOSE CLOSEST TO MY SOUL

To the man that is my hero and blueprint for becoming a true man

thank you for your sacrifice.

Without it, I would not be where I stand.

To the woman that is my guiding light and bearer of my life

thank you for your support.

Without it, I would be lost.

To the older sister that is my favorite trailblazer and teacher

thank you for your leadership.

Without it, I would not be a believer.

To the younger sister that is my first and favorite responsibility

thank you for your mere presence.

Without it, I would not know how to care.

To the baby that is my reminder of life's simple joys

thank you for your innocence.

Without it, I would forget my inner little boy.

WORDS TO THE WISE

Glances into the distance

as the views of an empty and hopeless dream neglect to reflect the voice
in which the deep beat continues to scream.

Words effortlessly flow off the top

conforming into the deceptive articulation whose maturation's illustration

is best defined as an excuse.

An illegitimate reason that only helps to console the fear of relentlessly
racing towards a destination whose end tape

can only be broken by the visionary who dares to chase it.

As the infinite light illuminates on life

assure yourself that your dreams become beams

unclouded by a forecast derived from an inner regime.

Never allowing the inevitable sunset to withhold regret

of a true

unformed GLEAM.

Dreamer's Prison Break

CONTENTS

INTRODUCTION

What's black without white

dark without bright

today without the sun

the moon without tonight.

What's a cat without a scratch

a dog without a bite

success without a plan

Better yet

a dream without sight.

What's falling without rising

two wrongs without a right

forever without "and ever"

marriage without plight.

What's good without bad

struggle without fight

life without love

love without life.

I don't know

I just hope these eyes that read what these words speak

will never allow the mouth of the ignorant

to tell these ears to listen to the simple minds of the weak.

It's never one

without the other.

Not in the darkest of nights

Nor in the brightest of days

Nothing's ever black and white

There's always

some GREYS.

HIM

Time ticks

and for the next 50 minutes my mind exits reality

entering the dimension of composition.

Ink travels without destination documenting all hopes and imagination.

In the real world

she's no more than a secret crush that sits 2 rows over and 4 seats up

but

on these pages bound by the outer black and white

admiring is no longer concealed

and is brought to the light.

In this world of fantasy

she bears my name

and *our* passion exceeds far beyond what words can acclaim.

Between these lines *she's* my only inspiration

and the fear of tears from never finding *her*

are mere evaporation.

From this pen lies love's freedom-key

to a world whose divine and endless blue surround *we*.

As the thoughts flow, script grows, papers turn

time reaches my desire's limitation with a simple ring.

Leaving endless thoughts

among my notebook DREAMS.

Closed eyes see the brightest skies.

I been thinking 'bout *you*

As the darkness of a cold and lonely world instantaneously

becomes a canvas that beholds

the art of *you.*

Never bestowed to the earth by the illustrations of paint

strokes of a brush

nor sprays of a can

but rather by the hands of someone that clearly understands an artistry

in which my eyes could never fathom

and one which my heart demands.

Though the spotlight of your greatness only glows when the lights go

your light shows.

Shows affection in a direction in which my blood flows

to the beat in which my heart knows.

So my love grows.

Grows with thoughts that this graceful angel incapable of flight can be mine.

A divine design

exuding a perfection and endless shine

Not bound by the ticks of a clock

nor by the hands of time.

So my love confides.

Confides in thoughts of cloud nine

with anticipation that our lives will soon intertwine

and in my arms

you'll soon reside.

Despite *your* beautification surpassing all explanation and justification

our relations

can only be found behind the walls of my mind's dreams.

Leaving my body wishful and hoping.

Hoping that the glorious figure I see will be there

when my eyes OPEN.

I love you.

At least that's what you wanted to hear.

So I used what you wanted

to get what I need.

I fed you lies to suppress your hunger

while I addressed my greed.

I'm who your heart wanted to trust

who your mind always feared

and who your soul tried to ban.

I'm the story teller

the dream seller.

I'm today's 'real' MAN.

Sun laid to rest

but your light glows in that sundress you used to outshine that star in the sky.

Now you're mine.

Well at least in the meantime.

It's fine.

It's selfish of me to get subjective and aggressive

over a selfless you

and it's childish of me to get obsessive and possessive

when that just ain't you.

It's fine.

My time is my time

and I know when tomorrow's nightfall calls your cell

it won't be from my line.

It's fine.

For now

just put your phone on lock and block your future.

Stay present and present your presence as a present

that only I could open.

It's fine.

I'm just hoping you would focus

and token my appreciation of monogamy

and lie with me.

Lie with me and lie to me

Lie to me

and tell me that your cherry-red lipstick leaves that stain only on my lips.

Lie to me

and tell me these goods I picked off the shelf in this aisle

were the last ones in the store and no one can purchase anymore.

Lie to me

Lie to me

and tell me that these eyes I'm staring into

only play this movie of eternity for me

and it's not on repeat.

Just lie to me

Lie to me and tell me that it's all mine.

Lie to me.

It's FINE.

As the night falls to rest and day awakens

her sea is revealed.

Green as nature's pastures

her eyes tell stories.

No glass slipper

No Prince Charming

No happily ever after

Just chapters.

Chapters of endless complexity and density

with the propensity to ward off

the incomprehension of the average reader.

Don't read *her*

see *her*.

See *her* art and *her* canvas

See *her* triumph and *her* pain

See *her* body and *her* mind

See *her* shine and *her* rain

Deeper than the ocean

Greener than the forest

Broader than the skies

Her body is the world's gift

and only a few

see *her* EYES.

Beautiful, gorgeous, flawless

you're this

impeccably drawn portrait

hanging in the ranks of Pablo

and though I can't afford this Picasso

I'll work these digits to the bone

if it means I have even the slightest chance to love *you* forever

in a home we call *our* fortress.

I'll compete all day and all night

with love, hate, and life

if at the end of my fight

you're what the award is.

You're my dedication turned nomination turned standing ovation

you

are my applause.

My beautiful conviction

If *you're* the crime, I'll do life with *you*

Long days turned longer nights with *you*

Do right by *you*

Even if it means doing all the wrong things

with my body in *yours*

all night with *you.*

My undeniable addiction

I get high off *you*

Overdosed on *your* light

I want to play husband and wife with *you*

Eternal life with *you.*

But before I jump too far ahead in calling *you* Mrs.

for now

less distance and more of *your* warm kisses

will DO.

Her mind is *her* illness

Poisoning competence

choking confidence

in a silhouette of promise.

Curable

by the slightest physical accomplishments

or constant compliments

her consciousness

can't seem to set *her* free.

Trapped behind the bars in *her* own head

she's a prisoner

with claustrophobia

confined between the lies that the court of society told *her*

defined beautiful.

Serving a life sentence with the possibility of parole

I'll be *your* lawyer.

I'll address the facts in this case which society deems suitable.

The evidence

the evidence is indisputable.

And no jury in this world can tell me any different

Your HONOR.

Pen and paper at hand

with a mind that knows it all

and a body that seems to never understand.

Confident in this ignorance I study and invest in

I continuously fail the test administered from this beat in my chest.

Unable to graduate from this class

I pass love notes to these severed dreams

as glances of this endless clock stream motion pictures of my future's

lost scenes.

She loves me

She loves me not

She loves me

but then *she* stops.

Contradiction addiction depicting clippings of outdated feelings

stripping the diction of my heart

and the truth of its benediction

crippling this happiness

which in me

was always MISSING.

I love

She lusts back

I stare

She glares back

Glances into empty eyes, with signs that no soul resides.

So to this body *she* confides

and in these tides I dive.

Lost for worth in this world

where concentration of these penetrations

overrides complications of my demise.

So these thighs I divide

and to *her* cries I provide.

Provide pleasure with this pain

and passion with this shame

but with these strokes

she cares not who I blame.

Her priorities comprised of the next man that lies inside

but to my oblige

what lies inside this domain referred to as "I"

implies not the lack of pride

but the lack of guide to find truth

in the life beside.

So down these unforgiving roads I stride.

Stride with hopes of outlasting plight

and these long nights turned longer days

next my light that shines under the sun.

Making that previous division of two

turn

a forever ONE.

Hand cuffed

and imprisoned in solitary

guarded by proportions of epic.

I won't let this

deflection direct the projection this love holds.

I won't accept it.

It's hectic.

Our lives connected and affected where the beat is

your soul shackled by shameful regret.

You object and neglect it

you won't accept it.

It's hectic.

Defenseless to those before me and obsessed with all of *you*

I won't let this

apprehended heart be acquitted of its truth.

I won't accept it

it's hectic.

But the moment *you* break free and accept *this*

I'll surrender to *your* ball and chain for life

leaving *our* cardiac

ARRESTED.

Lips with that MAC bliss locked on mine

while those hour glass hips

help pass the time.

I start my day with a sip of *your* coffee

and a taste of *your* breakfast.

Then go to work.

Hand over hand

I'm diligent with *your* task from 9 to 5

Then I leave.

Only to sit in *your* 6 o'clock traffic

never rushing the hour

nor neglecting *your* scene.

Then finally making it home

my daily ROUTINE.

Roses may show red

violets may grow blue

but the petals of a flower will never define the worth of *you*.

The divinity of the unappreciated stature

we call woman

is undermined by the physical blessings *she* protrudes

cloaking the priceless and undefined inner greatness *she* includes

among *her* perfect imperfections

only acknowledged by the courage and passion a true heart
exudes

so with this beat in my chest I let my words conclude...

You are

God's Vindication

beauty's Acclamation

dream's Limitation

perfect's Expectation

lost's Navigation

lust's Temptation

creativity's Inspiration

word's Narration

life's Explanation

and my mind always knew.

So down on one knee

I ask to spend my forever

with *YOU*.

From a young age we are introduced.

For most

such introduction entails a lack of knowledge and immature overlooking

of its powerful capabilities.

And in a world which possesses the inevitability of expiration

not all are blessed with its eternal association.

For those who are lucky enough to behold and embrace the gift of time

that once meaningless word now holds true definition.

And in a place where uncertainty and fear of never having it are a cancer

its cure will forever be *our* grasp.

So I ask…

Hold my hand

Through day and night

Hold it

So in darkness I have my light

Hold it

When my emotions run awry

Hold it

So in sadness my eyes stay dry

Hold it

And never let go

Hold it

So in doubt I'll always know

Hold it

When my water drops follow our grey skies

Hold it

So at *our* life's finish line I'll still have my prize

Hold it

As time stops and *our* hearts do the same

Hold it

So when my world aches I feel no pain

Hold it

As the words "I love" are followed by *you*

Hold my hand

And tell me "I DO."

As the heavenly ray pierces through the curtains

onto the golden that is

realization of sheer perfection becomes prevalent.

The peaceful aura encompasses the room

and true definition is discovered.

Perfection is Breathtaking

It is the slight shock of the body when *her* presence is near

Perfection is Striking

It is the instantaneous chill from *her* vocals I hear

Perfection is Heartbreaking

It is the small devastation brought on when *she* leaves

Perfection is Imagining

It is the insurmountable beauty brought on by *her* in my dreams

Perfection is Intriguing

It is the curiosity of how such divinity can be humane

Perfection is Astonishing

It is the exhilaration as *her* smile creates an angelic domain

Perfection is Staggering

And it is *HER*.

As the remnants of time

continue to fall through the cracks of notability of others

my apprehension of the wings bestowed upon the flight of time

will forever be envisioned by the absence of seconds

while I'm at the mercy of true infatuation.

In a second

My eyes witnessed perfection beyond fathom.

In a minute

My ears adopted a voice that surpassed astonishment.

In an hour

My hopes became the desire to call such artistry mine.

In a day

My mind discovered a new purpose to dream.

In a week

My life encompassed an unmatched significance.

In a month

My heart found true reason to beat.

In a year

My devotion was defined by the gold surrounding my very own jewel.

In a decade

My world revolved around an infant bearing her mother's beauty.

In an eternity

My love's clock continues to tick inside the heart

of *our* timeless PASSION.

My eyes close tight.

Eyelids holding one another in their efforts to avoid the nightmare

I witness when they open.

Open to a world in which the girl who once was my brightest light

now is an unknown figure

darker than the black I see with my eyes wide shut.

Behind these doors of darkness

lies the coldest images of *your* unforgivable fault.

Which evokes pain at its sharpest

denial at its hardest

and love at its farthest.

Now the distant person I see

is followed by the vision of infidelity and deceit.

Manufacturing a heart with no beat

and a voice unable to speak.

So I accept defeat.

Defeat in the battle of my mind

whose contemplations and complications continuously fail to conform

to the collaboration of *you* and I.

So I ask why.

Why would a person given anything and everything

long for the company of an eventual nothing.

But as my mind continues to ponder and question the coldest

soulless body that is *you*

I'll be sure to break through, and find comfort in a person

who will forever

stay TRUE.

Confrontation not with I

but *her* inner congregation of trust.

Incoherent to the words spoken from these lips

and the illustrations migrated from my heart

she tore us apart.

Confident in the lies

told by those on *her* side

she confides in the confines of a tainted mind.

Never mind the many times I try.

The addition of my positive efforts

are negated by those

you equate to be my equal.

So no solution

we FIND.

It's been a day.

And though 24 hours ago is close

time only multiplies when life divides.

Though love movies typically have happy endings

with my life coming to a complete standstill

there's clearly no positive emotion in this motion picture.

As time built

and distance grew

my only possessions were the mere memories *you* drew.

At the beginning of love's book

you're blinded by the imaginary sparks that flew

and all the fairytale dreams that seemingly came true.

Hiding the approaching disaster

that the two of you

never knew.

As words became weapons and love became hate

the only connection left

was the infamous drug of heartbreak.

Soon my addiction became overdose

scripting my final chapter

leaving no room

for *our* happily

ever AFTER.

HER

As the bell rings and control is no more

freedom becomes relevant

Flowing through the schoolyard

lacking care for all neglect and disinterest

Possessing attributes that can only be explained by its young beloved owner.

I see *you*

my heart stops, my body tingles, and my life changes.

From afar

your smile shows, *your* hair flows, and *your* world glows.

Still admiring from a distance

my stomach tightens, my dreams brighten, and my day lightens.

You see me

your cheek blushes, *your* blood rushes, all while my heart crushes.

You are

innocent, yet mature beyond *your* years

simple, yet convoluted in ways unimaginable

art, yet contain no canvas nor musical origin

selfless, yet embody more soul than life itself

embedded, yet freer than the air we breathe

a statement, yet bear no words or punctuation

timid, yet encompass an unmatchable pride

silent, yet express far beyond any vocabulary

ordinary, yet surpass all extraordinary barriers

my schoolyard love, yet somehow

I know

you're for ME.

The eyes of a guilty boy only notice such glow as a light.

One whose illumination is only noticed

when the sun falls

and the moon awakens the night.

But to an innocent man

the beautification of greatness is never conceived

by the optics of skin baring no cloth.

Nor is it perceived by the dreams of penetration

after the separation of my knees.

Still

in my innocent mind

innocent thoughts fluctuate through my less than innocent thighs

evoking man's guilty visions

and avoiding their sight of my innocent eyes.

But as nightfall calls for the company

of lonely and less than innocent measures

innocence wanders in the efforts of finding association

Typically ending in the acceptance of guilty pleasures.

Now my once youthful

innocent soul

is betrayed by my guilty body.

Infatuated with guilty aspirations

and temptations of physical relations

proceeding to guilty sensations.

Forever will the cases of my innocence be judged

by the assurance of my indulgent guilt that follows.

And in the rare incidence

that the elegance of my innocence

is not affiliated with guilty evidence

Know that my defense's relevance of decadence

will invariably be the verdict of governance.

Because in the court of life

we are all innocent

until proven GUILTY.

Vulnerable to the allure

the mind is intrigued by mystery.

Aware of possible expiration

temptation grabs the remote and presses play.

Hooked on every ounce of the movie

your heart grows fonder of its characters

neglecting the imminent credits at the END.

Long days full of hope of his return

and anticipation of his call

Only followed by struggle

of late-night pillow tears from clips of a man once here.

A man whose words I thought true

showing my heart sky blue

art my canvas never drew

and a future of "I do."

But as I fall deep

his words of infatuation

and thoughts of admiration

soon become the migration to the next willing to sleep.

So my love he won't keep.

Now I weep.

Weep until the puddle bound from my eyes

erases the lies of guys

who only find prize in the destination between my thighs.

Fated by the demise of my reputation of repetition

my soul cries.

Cries for truth in his voice and trust in my choice

that this one

this one will be everything I asked for

and will last past the point

in which the past became my last.

And the memories of the vast cast of men

will forever wither in their efforts

to surpass the class

that is *HIM*.

Different from any other

I stand convoluted and complete

Lacking the utmost suitable confidence

for the body that survives above my feet.

And like those lacking my physique

I trust the voice of my inner defeat

And though my esteem is low and weak

No sympathy I seek

Just silence

I SPEAK.

Eyelids latched together

imprisoning hope and locking down pain

I keep my windows locked

and doors closed

to avoid the rain

I've seen lightning

heard thunder

felt winds

Heart flooded

Mind blown away

Faith damaged

Foundation destroyed

I remember his terror

I've been through

a HURRICANE.

You say you love me.

I say liar.

I say you love what I am willing to do.

You say not true.

I say it's me who holds the key to that truth

not you.

It's the key that keeps us locked out of forever

The key that ignites my drive to find better

The key that plays our song

of never.

So I tune you out.

You and every other person only interested in playing my keys like Alicia.

To play this grand piano

You need to learn my intricacies

Understand my delicacies

And know my worth.

Without it

there is no MUSIC.

I've seen *your* movie

studied *your* scenes

memorized *your* plot.

Beginning to end

credits to credits

I understand

you.

I understand *your* controversy

Your foreshadows

your climax

your close.

Beginning to end

credits to credits

I understand

you.

What I never understand

is why the lead roles are never me

and *you.*

Cinemas aside

I never understood why *you* crave my affection.

Why *you* reach for my touch

never grasping my hand.

Why *you* see what *you* want

always looking past where I stand.

That

I'll never UNDERSTAND.

Stare into the mirror.

Close your eyes.

Close your eyes and picture.

Close your eyes and picture a flawless figure.

Now close your eyes and picture a flawless figure bound by the perfect
imperfections and angelic scriptures

that will always struggle to find the proper connection of words

to depict her

So pick her.

Pick her from the vast cast of women

who falter in their efforts to compare value in her worth

for in this game of life

her gorgeous nature

will never fall short of the unachievable first.

Still with your eyes closed

glance into the canvas of dark

and witness the unforgettable

and remarkable nature of her art.

Flowing strands wrapped around a glorious face

accented with heavenly white capable of impeccable illumination

in even the darkest of nights.

All powered by the strongest of hearts.

Now with your eyelids apart

Notice that your envisions of perfection fail to even come close

to the figure you saw at the start.

In part

forever will that dream fall by the wayside

and continually subside to the vision of the real woman

you now see with your eyes opened wide.

And for that

I hope you never forget that you are no man's possession

but rather his irreplaceable prize.

So always

open your EYES.

Thoughts of the uncontrollable fill this zone of comfort.

For years I've been just fine

doing and thinking about myself

personal success

inner peace

self-health

and future wealth.

But I forgot about *you*.

See I knew *you* would come

You were inevitable

Or at least that's how I saw it.

I never saw *you* in my own home

only in movies

felt *you* in songs

witnessed *you* in others.

I knew *you'd* come.

And in my maturation

my over-saturation of self-thought

turned into preparation for *you*.

I knew what *you* looked like

felt like

smelled like

sounded like

and even tasted like.

I knew *you*.

And then you CAME.

Can I stay awhile?

Can I stay

so that *you'll* know I never want to leave

long enough to allow these words I utter

to let *your* ears feel 'em and let *your* heart believe.

so that *your* grace places a blessing on mine

long enough to let the night's light turn a yellow shine.

so that *your* morning imperfections turn into my soul's daily desire

long enough to allow the girls of *your* prior

to become a distant past *you* no longer require.

so that this arithmetic proves true

long enough to allow the addition of *you* and division me

equal the multiplication of us

into a son that favors proof.

so that in a time of need *you're* all I see

long enough to allow "*Yours*" to become "*Ours*,"

"I's" become "*We's*,"

and together become eternity.

so that my "can I stay?" is replied by *your* "where are you going?"

long enough to allow the home of *your* care

to become the only place my love grows in.

So

can I STAY?

On the day of birth, it begins

And from that day forth

its life's path is foreseen by the continuity of its divine beginning.

Though in its creation

it bears no mind, apprehension, nor sight

its artistry is captured by a mere sensation.

To the customary person

its sole purpose is to work alongside others to provide a great cause.

But in reality

its true design lies within its continual exploration

for another

either greatly compatible or vastly incomparable.

To its students

its definition is categorized by science.

But to its teachers

it is defined by an undefined 4-letter word.

Though it has no hands

its angelic locksmith talents have continually sculpted the key

to the soul's most precious gift

of eternity.

Its unmatched force will forever be the impulse of life, and its key
components:

Passion, Pain, Strength, Weakness, Affection, Infatuation, Desire,

and LOVE.

Anger abated with the 26 flexed muscles activating serenity at its greatest.

2 creeks bound by flowers of the softest pink

accented with 32 pearls found by the wayside of the puddles

drowned in *his* cheeks.

Though its presence not eternal, the expedition to its existence will forever subjugate the ambition of my dream

and the ignition of my feet.

Regardless of the miles

my only purpose is to see *his* smile.

Serendipitous sensuality solidifying silence's

Majestic meaning. Molding memorable magic, matching

Intense infatuation inside

Love's

Everlasting embrace.

Smile.

Smile so that the brightest light in my world

outshines every star in the sky.

Smile so that the flawless heavens above

can maintain its aspiration of *your* perfection's most high.

Smile so that *your* incomprehensible nature gives mine description.

Smile so evoking *your* happiness

will always

be my MISSION.

As the night dies and sunrise awakens my eyes

I am yet again introduced.

Though such redundancy is overlooked

I never fail to see the truth.

Because the truth of what lies on the other side

is more than what meets the eye.

It is my light

And with it, my world is never dark.

It is my air

And without it, suffocation is inescapable.

It is my happiness

And with it, pain is nonexistent.

It is my voice

And without it, words bear no meaning.

It is my strength

And with it, weakness is irrelevant.

It is my dreams

And without it, sleepless nights are inevitable.

It is my success

And with it, failure is insignificant.

It is my heart

And without it, life is no longer.

It is *you*, my other side

And with *you*

I am COMPLETE.

Blessings Laid Upon Everything

my life could ever wish

without a genie in a bottle

or granter of my forever list.

Though blue is *his* truth

and it pumps red through my heart and veins

blue is never what he makes me

and *his* truth never induces pain.

Confused to whether *his* couth is to blame

or *his* youth to the game

ones thing's for certain

His blue is the only match for my delicate flame.

His glow admirable

His bliss unattainable

His beauty desirable

His grace inevitable

His color irreplaceable

His art memorable

His Blue Beautiful

His flow untouchable

His freedom unreachable

His love undeniable

His power unchallengeable

His music favorable

His words indefinable

His Blue Beautiful

His touch pleasurable

His pain forgivable

His scent lovable

His richness unbelievable

His originality unmatchable

His time untraceable

His Blue BEAUTIFUL.

Truthful body, but deceitful actions

Old sensations, but new attractions

Warmest blood, but the coldest heart

Same bed, but different parts

Shameless moans, but regretful skin

Caressing thoughts *you*, but with strokes of him

He was supposed to be my secret, but then you walked in.

They say…

There's a sucker born every minute

and at the end of the day

I was the one that found value in fool's gold.

From day one

with a heart of gold

you bent over backwards

and went the whole nine yards

for the fat chance

that these night-and-day lives we called "*us*"

could see eye-to-eye

from now until forever

and would love like there's no tomorrow.

I remember it like it was yesterday

an emotional roller coaster.

I fell head over heels

for this one in a million

once in a blue moon man

who finally put two and two together for me.

Not knowing what I had until it was gone

my Achilles heel

of trying to have my cake and eat it too

and expecting the grass to be greener on the other side

produced an end that is hard to swallow.

Swallowing my pride I understand

that with the game on the line

I fumbled *your* heart.

Now I wish upon a star.

In hopes that *you* realize that Rome wasn't built in a day

and there are no if's, and's, or but's about my wrongs.

They say...

Time heals all

and absence makes the heart grow fonder.

But I say...

I'm SORRY.

It took sleeping with him

and sleeping on *you* to realize

that sunsets

ain't got shit on *your* sunrise.

Heart knocking on *your* door outside

I stand before *you*

an imperfect woman

with swallowed pride inside

Praying *your* eyes are dried

and in *your* home *our* love still resides.

But to my surprise,

as *your* door opens

I'm greeted by the new me

My ultimate DEMISE.

Rubber worn out till bare skin shows and pain grows.

Lost soles from a lost soul

chasing destinations sold by imaginations of a fairytale.

Glorified animations of a life once capable

now favorable of the unattainable nonexistence

that glows in a sound distance.

So my body listens.

And without resistance

races towards the figment *your* open arms and loving heart

but as mine embraces

yours erases

and replaces my end with my start.

Rubber worn out till bare skin shows and pain grows.

Lost soles from a lost soul

chasing destinations sold by imaginations of a fairytale.

Glorified animations of a life once capable

now favorable of the unattainable nonexistence

that glows in a sound distance.

So my body listens.

And without resistance

races towards the figment *your* open arms and loving heart

but as mine embraces

yours erases

and replaces my end with my START.

Drifts into the open

as these doors hold closed and those hopes stay close.

Closed fists clench anger and hope

as this broken heart pilots these flights into my uncontrollable distance.

Distant from this reality I seek

Promise holds true that this grasp of everything will never grow weak.

Weeks generated from an accumulation of heartless days and selfish ways

with my tempted mind tainting *your* once glorious exuberance.

Guarding this cell of hate, regret, and pain

with keys that unlock this cage of infuriation and rage.

Engaged in these increasing gauges

I brace myself for impact and freedom

with thoughts of *us* that I can't erase.

Racing down this suicidal road into a bright white

my pedal to the floor

I promise to always keep my promise

of loving *you*

for forever MORE.

On the start of a journey

the road ahead holds promise and aspiration.

As inch after inch of asphalt is surpassed with grace and gratitude

the shortage of road holds no meaning.

For the youth

such expedition is solely for the sights along the way.

For the grown

expeditious travels are defined not by the world around

but rather the world right beside.

As mileage increases

and the start becomes distant

the once endless road now has a visible destination.

Time Rewinds.

Excitement brews, through visions of happiness under sky blues.

Smiles shine white, sun shines bright, as the bearings of the future hold

no fright.

Forever green pastures, uncontrollable laughter, as all signs point

'Happily Ever After.'

Then life switches gears, the end just appears, cheers become tears

and the mind

is unclear.

Present Time

Confusion grows, heartbreak shows, emotion flows, while the car

still goes.

World of clarity now haze, sky blues now greys, tragedy replays

and replays.

Heart still pacing, mind still racing, life memories retracing, *our* old life I'm
still chasing.

Depression severe, overdrive brings end near, and without fear…

I let go of the wheel.

Please take care of *our* baby girl

and know I will always love *you*

my DEAR.

THEM

Dear Time,

In my life you have been the second greatest gift that I have been given.

In a world full of change, you are the only thing I can count on.

You are consistent.

One tick after another in an effortless pace you chase my future.

You are persistent.

In most cases your remarkable diligence and progression to make me a better man is a gift worth holding forever, but in this case, I want to ask you a favor.

I ask that your strides come to a halt and retrace those of my past. See because in your journey you took my first gift. Something that coincidence and faith granted me years ago. I know this is a lot to ask for and many have done this before, but you have to believe me this is different. Just listen. Not to the desperation my vocal chords let out, but more importantly to the pain in which my heart can't shout. See, a little while ago, destiny decided to tear *us* apart and *we* counted on you to make sure everything would be fine. They told me you heal all, and that as long as I put my trust in you, these cardiac lacerations would close themselves. But it seems those words uttered to me you and you again only cut me deeper.

Please, I don't ask for much. I'm only asking that you rewind to the you when my eyes saw clarity thru the lens that was *her*. Take me back to the you, when eternity was the definition of *us*. Please, I don't ask for much. Just go back.
Back to the you when the smile between her cheeks was as bright as the glow of *her* soul when she held my presence.

Just give me this one present. Leave the present and present me with the history my happiness is so fond of. Because my future can't seem to find that love.

You changed *her*. You took *her* from me. Induced *her* pain at night. Told *her* tears she was okay without me. Told *her* mind I didn't care. Told *her* body I didn't need it. Didn't want it, and that *she* could do better.

Please. I don't ask for much.

All I ask

is that you bring back

my FOREVER.

Flashes of the end on repeat

as I wait in this waiting room

with no room left for the blossoms of *your* forgiveness to bloom

and no time left to wait in this room plagued by doom.

Doomed and paralyzed by the demise in *your* temptation and lost pride

waiting here in this very same waiting room.

My helpless vessel and racing mind wrestles the idea of how one mistake

erased everything.

One is all it takes to bring our pain

manifest our rain

and take the soul my body once claimed.

So as my last cry

for the many tears I've shed

and a joyful passion turned dead

I pray that peace is what *you* attain.

I pray that soon

I find selflessness in this selfish world

And more than anything

I pray the Lord brings back life

in *our* lifeless little girl.

She was never supposed to get in between *our* failures

or endure *our* pain.

She was *our* greatest proof

that *our* love was ordained.

She had *our* beauty. *Our* blood.

She had *our* veins.

She was supposed to outlive the both of *us*

and be the rose that grew from *our* concrete.

Not die in vain.

But as I open my eyes

to this unchartered terrain

a doctor replies

both of *your* souls were lost in that crash.

And *your* lives

no longer REMAIN.

Far too often does the mind make accommodations

lacking crucial pause and definite cause

leaving the rest of the body to play victim

without probable cause.

Decisions never made by absence of vision

but rather realistic foresight

ultimately ending in wishful views of insight.

Despite the feelings that linger in hindsight.

Clarity of life was never meant by the eyes of see-through

But rather the ones that see through its flaw

see past its awe

which blueprints an end

without the heart's withdraw.

Forever will the greatest destruction of existence

be the construction of the mistakes

and mishaps for those

who fail to realize that true angelism

cannot be found

in those bound by the conceptional abode above,

but rather the earth's exceptional home of love.

And in the end,

only foolery can define

dismay of those

who continue to follow angels

that continue

to FLY AWAY.

ABOUT THE AUTHOR

To comprehend I

is to conceptually deliberate a city

whose concrete jungle filled with relentless lions

never fails to shape the animal that lies inside

awaiting its chance to surprise the eyes of all skepticism

that resides in the hearts

in which a hater confides.

To envision I

is to visually decipher a city

whose skyline's endless shine enables

the continual dreams of inner illumination

establishing a reincarnation of greatness

never introduced to life's orchestration.

To receive I

is to perceive and explain a city

whose design encompasses an unattainable and unexplainable swagger

not bound by any brand of cloth or threads surrounding my skin

but rather drowned in the profound mind within.

To know I,

Is to know that the human product

whose inconsistent consistency which stands in front

was incapable of existence without the assistance

of the proud city

that forever

stands BEHIND.

www.ingramcontent.com/pod-product-compliance
Lightning Source LLC
Chambersburg PA
CBHW052016170626
46808CB00007B/2953